Word List

Here is a list of words that might make it easier to read this book. You'll find them in boldface the first time they appear in the story.

nervous	NER-vus
scientists	SY-uhn-tists
trophies	TROH-fees
experiments	eks-PER-uh-ments
tadpoles	TAD-polz
acid rain	AS-id RAYN
harmony	HAR-muh-nee
ecosystem	EK-oh-sis-tum
terrarium	tah-RAIR-ee-um
cooperating	koh-OP-uh-rayt-ing
environment	en-VY-ruhn-ment
ballot	BAL-uht
civic center	SIV-ik SEN-ter
incubators	ING-kyuh-bay-terz
electric current	I-LEK-trik KER-rent
congratulations	kuhn-GRACH-uh-LAY-shunz
celebrate	SEL-uh-brate
recycling	ree-SY-kul-ing
community	kuh-MYOO-nuh-tee

The Class Act

©1998 Mattel, Inc. Barbie and associated trademarks are owned and used under license from Mattel, Inc. All Rights Reserved. Published by Grolier Enterprises, Inc. Story by Rita Balducci. Photo crew: Scott Fujikawa, Mary Reveles, Glen Bradley, Peer Johnson, and Judy Tsuno. Produced by Bumpy Slide Books.
Printed in the United States of America.

ISBN: 0-7172-8798-X

Grolier Books

Chapter One

It was the first day of the school year. Barbie drove into the school parking lot and parked her car. She couldn't wait to start her job as the new fifth-grade teacher. She was a little **nervous**, though.

First she went to the principal's office.

"Good morning, Principal Gayle," said Barbie.

"Good morning, Barbie," said the principal. "Are you ready to meet your new students?"

"I think so," said Barbie. "I just hope the children like me as much as I liked *my* fifth-grade teacher. I'll never forget how she taught me to love science!"

"Don't worry," Principal Gayle told Barbie. "I'm sure you'll do fine."

"I hope you're right!" said Barbie.

"Well, if you run into any problems, please come see me," said Principal Gayle. "My door is always open!"

Barbie smiled. "I sure hope that won't be necessary," she said. "When I went to school here, I did my best *not* to end up in the principal's office!"

Principal Gayle laughed. Then Barbie took a deep breath and went down the hall. She walked into her classroom and looked around. Before long it would be filled with her new students. She had spent the week before putting up colorful posters and mobiles. She thought the room looked great. The windowsills were lined with plants. The shelves were filled with books. In one corner was a huge fish tank.

Soon the bell rang, and the school day began. Barbie waited in front of her desk. As the students came into the room, Barbie gave them a bright smile. After the children took their seats and quieted down, she introduced herself.

"I will be your teacher for this year," Barbie began. "I'm looking forward to getting to know each of you. I hope we'll learn a lot together and also have a lot of fun!"

After Barbie took attendance, she began to pass out books.

"I thought we'd begin today with a science lesson," she said.

A boy in the back of the room slumped down in his seat and yawned. Barbie smiled right at him and kept talking.

"Science is one of my favorite subjects," Barbie began.

A brown-haired girl sitting in the front row

whispered to her friend, "Yuck! I think science is boring."

"Yeah," her friend agreed.

Barbie heard them. "I know some of you think science is boring. But it's not. Science is part of all of our lives," Barbie said.

"What do you mean?" asked a girl.

"Well, what are some things you all enjoy doing?" Barbie asked.

"Sleeping and eating!" the yawning boy called out. The class giggled.

"Very good examples!" Barbie said. "Sleep helps repair our bodies, and food gives us energy. Not only that, but many **scientists** study the meaning of dreams! And dreams are an important part of sleep. What else do you like?"

The boy looked surprised. "Well, I guess I like music," he said.

"Another great example of science at work," said Barbie. "This year we'll learn about sound and how the ear works. We'll also learn how different insects make their own sort of music. By the way, I like music, too."

The boy smiled at Barbie.

Before long all the students were raising their hands and talking. Soon Barbie learned that the boy in the back row was named Mark. She also found out that he loved to skateboard. A girl named Emma sat in the front row. She liked to collect butterflies and other insects. There were also twins in the class. Their names were Sara and Kara and they liked skiing and hiking. Another student named Dave loved fishing. And a student named Annie liked flowers and plants.

"Believe it or not, science can help you with all those things," Barbie told her students. "Now do you see what I mean about science being fun?"

Barbie was happy that everyone seemed to be enjoying the class. For the next hour, she and her students talked about what they had learned in fourth-grade science. They also talked about what else they would be studying during the year.

After a while, it was time to move on to other subjects. At the end of the day, Barbie was tired but happy. "It looks like this class will be a lot of work but a lot of fun, too," she thought.

Chapter Two

A few weeks later, Barbie stood in front
of the class. "I have exciting news, class!" she
began. "There's going to be a science fair for all
the elementary schools in the area. Three **trophies**
will be awarded within each grade. I thought it
might be fun for you to try doing your own
science **experiments** for the contest. It will help
you learn what it's like to be real scientists."

"What would we have to do?" a boy named
Mike asked.

"Well, first we would have a few lessons on
how to set up a science experiment," Barbie

explained. "Then you could do any project you want. Pick something you're interested in. You could work alone or in teams. I have books with lots of ideas for science projects."

"Then what would happen?" Mike asked.

Barbie replied, "Each team or person could present a project to the class. Then the class could vote on which project will go to the fair. It will be like having our own mini science fair! What do you say?"

"When can we begin?" a girl in the front row wanted to know.

"Yeah, sounds like fun!" someone else added.

Barbie laughed. "How about today?" she suggested.

The students thought that was a great idea.

As Barbie talked, she handed out the facts on the contest. "We have six weeks to work on the projects," she explained. "I'm here to help you, so don't be shy about asking questions!"

But Barbie didn't need to worry. None of her students was shy. All at once, hands shot up around the room.

"Can I bring in my hamster?" asked Kara.

"Where can I buy some sea monkeys?" asked Dave.

"Does the report have to be typed?" Mark worried.

"I don't know what to do!" declared Emma.

Barbie patiently answered all her students' questions. Then she spent the next few science classes teaching them how to set up experiments. By the end of the week, everybody knew what he or she wanted to do. Most of the students decided to work in teams with their friends. Others preferred to work by themselves. Mark said that he wanted his project to be a surprise.

The following Monday when Barbie was starting class there was a knock on the classroom

door. Principal Gayle came into the room. She was followed by a new student. The girl had long, red hair and glasses.

"Class, I'd like you to meet Jane," the principal said. "It's her first day at our school. I know you will make her feel welcome."

"Hi, Jane," said Barbie. "Welcome to our class."

After Principal Gayle left, Jane smiled shyly at Barbie.

"We're working on our projects for the science fair just now. On the first day of school we learned how science plays a part in our everyday lives," Barbie went on. "What kinds of things are you interested in?"

Jane was not used to all the attention. She cleared her throat and softly said, "Um, I like animals."

"Great!" Barbie said. "This year we're going to study all types of animals. We might even have some friendly pets to keep in our class. I think you'll like it here."

Jane looked down at her feet. Barbie saw that her new student was shy.

"Why don't you take that empty seat in the second row?" said Barbie.

Jane nodded and sat down.

"All right, class," Barbie said as she sat behind her desk. "I would like all of you to tell Jane a little bit about your science projects. Then Jane can decide what she would like to do."

After they were finished, the bell rang. It was time for recess. The children grabbed their snacks. They quickly headed out the door. Barbie noticed Jane still sitting in her seat.

"The playground here is great," Barbie told Jane. "Aren't you going to take a look?"

"I guess so," Jane said. "But I don't have any friends here."

"Well, why not just walk up to someone

and say 'hi'?" Barbie asked.

Jane looked nervous.

"Come on, I'll give you the grand tour," said Barbie. "Then we can walk to the school yard together."

Jane was glad that someone was showing her around the school. Barbie found out that Jane's old school was much smaller. Barbie knew it was hard to switch to a new school. She understood that Jane missed her old friends.

After the tour of the school was over, Jane looked at Barbie and said, "Thanks." Then she surprised Barbie with a bright smile.

Barbie smiled back and said, "Sometimes it's a little scary being new."

Jane nodded.

"You know," Barbie said, "I'm new at being a teacher."

"Really?" Jane said in surprise.

"Really," said Barbie. "But I've always

found that once you start sharing things you enjoy with other people, it's easier to make friends."

They reached the school yard and Barbie saw some of her students playing kickball.

"Emma! Sara! Annie!" called Barbie. The three girls walked over to Barbie and Jane.

"Could you use another person to play kickball?" Barbie asked them.

"Sure," said Annie. She looked at Jane and smiled.

"Have fun," Barbie said to them. "I'll see you in a little while."

"Bye," said Jane, waving good-bye.

Later, Barbie thought about Jane and how hard it is to fit in. "Maybe she feels nervous about joining one of the science project teams," Barbie said to herself. "She might feel better doing a project on her own."

So at the end of class the next day, Barbie

called Jane over to her desk. "Have you decided which science project you'd like to do?" Barbie asked her.

"Well, I was thinking about doing something with my pet frog, Fred," Jane said softly.

"That's a good idea," said Barbie.

"Maybe I could bring in Fred and some **tadpoles**. Then I could show how tadpoles grow into frogs," Jane said quietly.

"Terrific!" said Barbie. "That sounds like it would make a great project!"

"I don't know," Jane said. "It might not be good enough. Maybe I'll do something else."

Barbie shook her head. "I love the frog idea," she declared. "And the rest of the class will, too."

"You really think so?" Jane asked.

"I sure do," Barbie declared.

Jane thought for a moment. "Okay," she replied. "I guess I could give it a try."

"Good!" said Barbie. "You can check out one of the classroom books to get some facts on tadpoles and frogs. Besides, next month we're going to study animals. Your project would be a big help!"

"Neat!" said Jane. She gave Barbie a big smile and skipped out of the classroom.

Chapter Three

For the next few weeks, Barbie's students worked hard on their projects. They couldn't wait until the final twenty minutes of each day. That's when they could discuss their ideas and ask Barbie questions. They were having so much fun! Barbie was having fun, too. And even though Jane was still shy, she seemed to be smiling more and more.

"She just needs a little more confidence," Barbie thought. "I hope this project helps!"

At last the week came for everyone to show the class what he or she had been working on. The classroom was buzzing with excitement.

"Okay, who would like to go first?" Barbie asked the class.

Annie and two other girls raised their hands. The girls carefully walked to the front of the classroom. They each carried a tray holding a paper cup. Each cup had a small plant growing out of it.

"Our project shows that plants will always grow toward light," Annie began. "We planted a bean seed in each of these cups. Then we put them in a sunny spot and kept the soil damp. When the plants had grown a few inches high, we put two of the cups on their sides. Soon the plants began to curve around the rims of the cups. See how they grew up toward the sun."

"Terrific!" said Barbie. "Nice work!"

Annie and her team answered questions on their project. Then the girls made their way back to their seats as everyone clapped.

"Next?" Barbie called.

Mark raised his hand. "Me! Me! Me!" he shouted.

Barbie nodded. Mark marched to the front of the room. There was a brown bag in his hand.

"Most of us have five senses: hearing, seeing, smelling, touching, and tasting," he said. "Today I am going to talk about the wonderful world of taste and how it makes our lives so, uh, tasty!"

The class giggled. Mark smiled and went on.

"Everybody, stick out your tongues, like this," he said. "There are thousands of tiny little bumps on the tongue called taste buds. Each group of taste buds tastes something different."

Mark reached into the paper bag and pulled out a plastic bag of chocolate candy. Then he pulled out a large plastic bag full of lemon slices. "I'd like everyone to come up and take one piece of chocolate and one slice of lemon," he said. As the other students gathered around, he continued.

"We are going to decide which is better, the sweet buds or the sour buds. Eat up!"

Soon the class was gobbling down the chocolate and throwing out the lemons. The sweet taste buds won, hands down.

"All right, everyone, please return to your seats," Barbie said.

Mark grinned at his teacher. "Not a bad project, huh? Now that I've given out candy, I bet everyone will vote for my project to go to the science fair!"

Barbie had to smile at Mark's project. "Oh, well," she told herself. "Maybe they did learn a tiny bit of scientific information from that."

It took until the end of the week before all the projects had been presented. Kara's team explained how fruit rots. They brought in some baker's yeast and showed how it can make bananas turn brown and moldy. Emma's team brought in some crickets to show how the insects chirp by rubbing their legs together.

Unfortunately, some projects did not work out as well. Sara tried to show the effects of **acid rain** on plants. But she didn't realize that it can take months of acid rain for leaves to turn brown. So when she poured her mixture on the plants, nothing happened. Dave tried to prove how smart caterpillars were by getting them to do tricks. But the bugs just crept across Barbie's desk and into her lunch bag.

At last, on Friday, it was Jane's turn.

"Okay, Jane. Tell us about your project," Barbie said. Jane nervously carried a jar and a square glass box to the front of the room.

In the jar were three tadpoles. Jane reached inside the glass box and pulled out Fred, her frog.

"Gross!" cried a few of the students.

"Jane is going to get warts," whispered another student. A few of her classmates giggled. Jane frowned.

"Okay, now, let's all settle down and listen to Jane," said Barbie.

"This is Fred. He's a desert frog," Jane began. "He isn't gross and he doesn't give you warts."

But before Jane could continue, Fred leapt right out of her hands.

"EEEK!" screamed Sara.

"Look out!" yelled Dave.

The frog landed on a desk in the front row. Then it jumped onto the floor and started hopping around everyone's feet.

"Oh, no!" cried Jane. "Careful, don't step on him!"

Meanwhile, everyone was shouting and laughing.

"All right, class," Barbie said. "Quiet down while Jane catches our runaway guest."

At last, Jane cornered the frightened animal. "Come on, Fred," she said softly, "let me put you back where you'll be safe."

Barbie waited until Jane had the frog safely back in its glass box.

"Okay, Jane," Barbie said calmly. "Please continue."

This time Jane left Fred in his container. She quietly began to explain how tadpoles turn into frogs. But by that time it was hard for the class to settle down. Barbie had to quiet everyone in order for Jane to be heard.

Then the bell rang.

"Oh, look at the time!" cried Barbie. "Now don't forget. On Monday we'll vote on which project should go to the science fair. So your only homework this weekend is to think about which project you want to vote for."

"All right!" said a few of the students.

"See you all next week!" said Barbie as her students grabbed their lunch boxes and jackets.

"Sorry about your project, Jane," said one

of the children.

"Yeah, too bad," said another. "But you know, you're right. Frogs aren't gross. They're really pretty cool."

Soon everyone was gone. Jane just sat at her desk staring at her frog.

Barbie gave Jane a kind look. "I'm very proud of you," she told Jane. "It wasn't easy to continue with your talk even though your project . . . " Barbie thought for a moment.

"Was a disaster?" Jane said.

"No," stated Barbie. "It just didn't go as planned. And remember that some of the other kids' projects didn't go that well either. But you made the best of it."

"Thanks," said Jane. "I just wanted to show everybody how amazing animals are. Did you know that every animal has a purpose all its own?" Jane asked.

"Yes, and I believe that the students who

could *hear* you today, Jane, learned that, too," replied Barbie.

"I hope so," said Jane.

"No matter what project goes to the fair, the most important thing is that everybody learns and tries," said Barbie.

"I guess you're right," said Jane. "See you on Monday!"

Over the weekend, Barbie thought about her students' projects. All of the projects were good. But Barbie knew her students could do something even bigger and better.

She went on a picnic with Ken and talked to him about her class. "I feel like there's something more that we could do for the science fair," she told him.

Together they watched a flock of birds fly overhead in a perfect V.

"Well, you're always saying how everything in nature works together in **harmony**," said Ken.

"It sounds to me like your class could use a little of that."

"What a great idea, Ken!" said Barbie. "Instead of picking one student's project for the science fair, we could combine all the projects into one big one!"

"Glad I could help," Ken said. "Now let's work together on eating these sandwiches. I'm starving!"

"Another good idea!" said Barbie, laughing.

They enjoyed the rest of the afternoon in the park. Barbie couldn't wait until Monday to tell her class about her new idea!

Chapter Four

On Monday morning, Barbie greeted her class with a huge smile. "All of your projects from last week were very good," she told them. "However, I have an idea of how to make them even better. I checked the rules for the contest again. I found out we can enter a project done by the whole class. So I thought we could put together parts from all the projects. Then we could make the parts into an **ecosystem**!"

Dave raised his hand. "What's that?" he asked.

"Well," explained Barbie, "an ecosystem

is a group of living things and the place in which they live. Hopefully, they all exist together in harmony. This means that every living thing has its own purpose but helps many other things."

Barbie winked at Jane. Jane smiled back at her.

"We can create our own little ecosystem in class," said Barbie. "Then we'll watch it grow and change."

"Wow!" said Emma.

"That sounds cool!" added Mark.

"It's going to take a lot of teamwork," Barbie told them. "But I know we can do it. What do you think?"

"Sounds great!" the class cheered.

"Okay, let's have a look at all of our projects," Barbie said.

She picked up a piece of chalk. Then she wrote a name for all the projects up on the board. "Plants, crickets, a frog, mold, candy . . . " Barbie read down the list.

Jane raised her hand.

Barbie called on her. "Yes, Jane?"

"Well, um," said Jane softly, "I read a chapter from one of your books on ecosystems. And almost everything on our list can be put in a **terrarium**."

"Good idea!" said Barbie. "A terrarium would make a perfect mini-ecosystem. In fact I think there's even an empty fish tank in the school's storage closet."

Actually, finding the fish tank was easy. Getting everyone to work together was a bit trickier. The students disagreed on how to set up the terrarium, and then they couldn't agree on what to write in the report.

"We're trying to show how things live in harmony," Barbie reminded her students. "It would be a good idea to practice some harmony ourselves."

But with Barbie's help, her students were soon **cooperating**. Whenever they disagreed, they would discuss it. Then they would vote to decide what to do next. Everyone was having lots of fun, and they were making progress, too.

Chapter Five

Little by little, the science project began to fall into place. After much talking and planning, the students knew what to do. First, they placed soil at the bottom of the tank and added some plants and rocks. Then, they planted some of the bean seeds from Annie's team. They added Dave's caterpillars and crickets from Emma's project. Next, Kara's team put in some of its mold. Sara and her team made a stronger acid rain mixture. Parts of the other projects were added as well. The only thing left was Mark's candy.

"What should we do?" Annie asked Barbie. "Candy isn't part of an outdoor **environment**."

Then Emma spoke up. "No, but candy wrappers sometimes are!" she said. "The other day my dad and I were taking a walk and we saw some in the woods. So we picked them up to help the environment."

"Good thinking!" Barbie answered. "Let's add the wrappers as an example of littering."

Mark grinned. "See! I told you my project was scientific!"

Everyone laughed, including Jane. She was having a lot of fun working on the class project. She had learned a lot, too, and not just about science. She was getting to know her classmates. She found out that a few of the other students shared some of her interests. With each day, Jane was feeling less shy. She even began to speak up in class.

Barbie was happy to see the changes in

Jane. One afternoon when the bell rang, Barbie called Jane over to her desk.

"Feeling more at home lately?" Barbie asked Jane.

Jane grinned. "Yes," she told her teacher. "You were right. Lots of kids like animals, too. And talking about something I like has made it easier to make friends. In fact I was even invited to a birthday party today."

"That's great, Jane," Barbie said with a warm smile.

"Do you think our project will win a prize at the fair?" asked Jane.

Barbie thought for a moment. "Every school in the county will be entering the contest," she said to Jane. "I think we have a good chance. And winning a trophy would be nice. But the best thing is that we all learned how to work together to make it happen."

Finally the ecosystem was finished. The

Homework

Math – Page 42
#1-10

History – Chapter 3
Answer review
questions 1-4

whole class was proud of it. The terrarium was filled with plants, insects, mold, a small dish of water, Fred the frog, and even a few candy wrappers. It looked like a miniature park!

"Great job, class!" Barbie told her students. "Now only one step remains. We need to elect one student to present the project and answer the judges' questions. Everyone write down the name of the person you think will do the best job. Then drop your **ballot** in the box that is being passed around the room."

Soon the ballot box was full. Sara brought it up to Barbie's desk. Barbie took out the pieces of paper. She sorted the papers into piles and counted each of them.

"And the lucky student is . . . Jane!" Barbie said out loud.

Everyone clapped loudly. Jane blushed with surprise.

"Thank you," said Jane. "I promise I'll do

the best I can!"

After class, Jane talked with Barbie about the science fair.

"Are you excited?" Barbie asked her.

"Yes, and a little nervous," Jane said. "But I was much more nervous that first day I walked in here!"

"A lot has happened since then," Barbie reminded her.

Jane nodded and smiled. "You're right," she said. "You know, I was wondering if you could write down some of the questions the judges might ask. That way, I could start to practice what I'm going to say."

"That's a good idea," said Barbie. "We can begin going over it on Monday."

"Great!" said Jane. "See you then!"

All the following week, Jane practiced answering questions in front of the whole class. After so much practice and help from the other students, Jane felt she was ready for the presentation. In fact, she couldn't wait.

Chapter Six

Finally the big day arrived. Barbie and her class took a school bus to the science fair.

Barbie and Jane rode in the front to keep an eye on the terrarium. Barbie told Jane, "We don't want to take any chances with the terrarium tipping over. Whatever you do, hold on tight!"

"You can count on me!" Jane replied.

The science fair was held at the **civic center**. The bus pulled into the parking lot.

"Well, this is it!" said Barbie to her students.

Carefully she and Jane carried the terrarium off the bus. Then they made their way through the busy crowd. The civic center was packed with teachers, students, parents, and local news reporters. At last, Barbie and her class made it to their school's table.

"Easy does it," Barbie said as she placed the terrarium on the table.

The fifth graders were not going to be judged until later that afternoon. Barbie and her students spent the morning looking at all the other science projects.

The science fair had many displays. There were ant farms and **incubators** filled with fuzzy yellow chicks. They saw a solar system made of tennis balls spinning in circles. A skeleton of plastic bones made Emma jump back in surprise.

"Hey, everybody! Look at this!" shouted Mark. He pointed to an **electric current** running between two potatoes. "A *third*-grade student did that!" he exclaimed.

"Some of these projects look pretty good,"

Jane said to Barbie with a frown. "It's going to be tough."

"Yes, they do *look* good," Barbie said. "But how they look is only part of it. The judges' questions are important, too. The students talking about the projects have to know their stuff."

"I guess you're right," said Jane.

"Besides," said Barbie, "our ecosystem looks fantastic! And I know you'll answer the judges' questions just fine. I'm not worried at all."

"Oh, I'm not worried, either," Jane said quickly. Then she paused. "Well, maybe a little."

At last it was time for the fifth-grade judging. Barbie fixed the terrarium for the hundredth time. Dave and Sara helped Jane practice answering questions. Slowly, all of her classmates began to gather around the table to watch.

"Here come the judges," Barbie said as a group of people walked up to their display.

Jane gulped and wiped her sweaty palms on

her dress. Barbie patted her on the shoulder. "You'll be fine," Barbie told her.

"Good afternoon," Jane began, smiling at the judges. "We're the fifth-grade class from Green Hills Elementary School. Today I would like to explain how our terrarium ecosystem works."

One of the judges smiled. Jane smiled back and relaxed a little.

"We have created our own ecosystem, with water, air, plants, and other living things. Placed together, all these things have an effect on one another. For example, the water helps the plants grow, and the insects eat the plants."

As Jane explained the ecosystem, Barbie watched the judges. She could tell by their faces that Jane was doing a great job.

Now it was time for the judges to ask questions. Her classmates held their breath as Jane calmly and clearly answered every question

GREEN HILLS
ELEMENTARY SCHOOL

that was asked. Then she invited the judges to look at the terrarium more closely.

"Very interesting," said one of the judges.

Another one asked, "So everything inside depends on everything else that's in there?"

"Yes," Jane said. "It's a perfect example of working together. In fact it works for people, too. This project was a group effort. Our whole class worked on it."

Her classmates looked on proudly.

The judge smiled. "There's no better way of doing things."

The presentation was finally over. Now everyone could relax and wait for the final results. They crossed their fingers as the judges moved on to the next display.

"Whew!" Jane said with relief. "Do you think they liked it?"

"I think they LOVED it!" Barbie exclaimed. "What do you think, class?"

The other students gave Jane a round of applause. They all told her what a great job she had done. Barbie was thrilled.

Chapter Seven

At last it was time to present the awards for the fifth-grade projects. The judges began with awarding the prize for third place. Barbie and her class were nervous and excited. Only two more prizes to go!

"And the second prize goes to . . ." the judge said, "Green Hills Elementary's fifth-grade class!"

Barbie and her students cheered. Their project had won a prize! The judges came over and placed a shiny trophy right in front of the terrarium.

"**Congratulations**, everyone!" Barbie said. "I'm really proud of the work you did. Wait until Principal Gayle finds out. She's going to be so proud!"

When they got back to school, Principal Gayle placed the trophy in the display case outside her office. The next day, she had ice cream delivered so the whole school could **celebrate**. There was even a banner hanging in Barbie's classroom that read "Congratulations."

While Barbie's students ate their ice cream, Principal Gayle came over to them. She was holding the local newspaper.

"Look, everyone!" Principal Gayle exclaimed. "Your picture is in the newspaper!"

The whole class gathered around to see. Sure enough, there was Barbie's class standing next to the trophy with the judges.

Barbie read the article out loud to the class. All the students' names were listed.

CONGRATULATIONS!

"Wow!" said Kara. "We're famous!"

"You all deserve it!" Barbie told her students. "You did a great job!"

"Gee, now that the science fair is over, what are we going to do for the rest of the year?" Annie asked.

Barbie smiled. "I was wondering that myself," she said. "Since our terrarium works so well, it seems a shame to put it away."

"What do you mean?" Mark asked.

"Well, yesterday on the way home, I had an idea," Barbie explained. "We don't want to forget everything we've learned, right? So why don't we expand our project to protect our own environment? We could tell other students about ecosystems. Then we could let them know how they can help the ecosystem right where they live."

"You mean things like **recycling**?" Kara asked.

"Exactly," said Barbie. "At each meeting,

we can focus on many of the problems facing the environment. We'll come up with different ways we can improve our own ecosystem, right here in Green Hills."

"I want to clean up that creek in the park," said Dave. "My dad said he used to fish there. I'd like to fish there someday, too."

"Well, I think we should start a **community** vegetable garden," Annie declared. "We could donate the food to a charity."

"Those are wonderful ideas," said Barbie.

Jane was so busy writing, she hadn't said a word.

"Jane, what do you think?" Barbie asked.

"I think we should write down everybody's ideas," she said with a smile. "Then we could tell everyone in town what we're doing in a newsletter!"

"That's the spirit!" said Barbie.

"It'll take a lot of work," said Jane, "but I

think it'll be fun. We'll need people to write the articles, people to make copies, people to fold the newsletter, and people to deliver it."

Barbie laughed. "Well, class, it looks like our own ecosystem is about to become a lot busier!"